BY MICHAEL ANTHONY STEELE

ILLUSTRATED BY PAULINE REEVES

raintree

a Capstone company — publishers for children

Raintree is an imprint of Capstone Global Library Limited, a company incorporated in England and Wales having its registered office at 264 Banbury Road, Oxford, OX2 7DY – Registered company number: 6695582

www.raintree.co.uk
myorders@raintree.co.uk

Designed by Ted Williams
Design Elements: Shutterstock: Angeliki Vel, MAD SNAIL, nazlisart
Original illustrations © Capstone Global Library Limited 2019
Originated by Capstone Global Library Ltd
Printed and bound in India

ISBN 978 1 4747 5827 7
22 21 20 19 18
10 9 8 7 6 5 4 3 2 1

British Library Cataloguing in Publication Data
A full catalogue record for this book is available from the British Library.

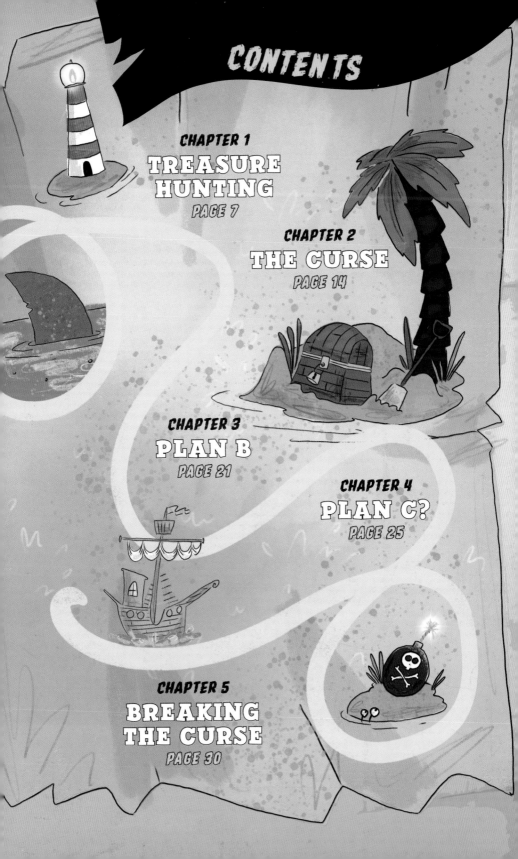

CONTENTS

MEET THE CREW

CAPTAIN BANANA BEARD

Captain Banana Beard is the almost brave leader of the monkey pirates. Banana Beard often puts his search for treasure before the safety of his crew. But he always gives credit where credit is due!

FIRST MATE FEZ

Wearing a red fez hat (I wonder how he got his name?), Fez is in charge of the ship's charts and books. He tries to keep Captain Banana Beard's plans from getting too crazy, but that's a nearly impossible job for any monkey!

BANANAJUICE

BANANAS

CREWMAN MR PICKLES

Mr Pickles is the lowest on the chain of command, but he still tries to be the best pirate he can be. With every job he does, Mr Pickles is one step closer to being a great pirate captain, just like his hero – Captain Banana Beard.

QUARTERMASTER FOSSEY

Fossey keeps track of the ship's goods and treasure. She's in charge of all the equipment and knows the supplies down to the last banana. And if the adventure calls for a certain tool that the ship doesn't have, Fossey can build it in record time.

COCO NUT OIL

CHAPTER 1

TREASURE HUNTING

Captain Banana Beard leaned over the ship's railing. Bubbles rose from the water below.

"What's the yo-ho-hold-up?" he asked his crew.

Fez and Fossey worked furiously nearby. The monkeys took turns pulling and pushing wooden handles up and down.

The handles were part of one of Fossey's machines. This machine pumped air through a long hose leading into the water.

"It's . . . a big . . . ocean . . . Captain," Fez said between breaths.

Banana Beard shook his head. "When I was but a young scallywag, I would have found some treasure by now."

"He's been . . . down there . . .
all day," Fossey added.

"Argh," growled the captain.
"Pull him up then."

Fossey sprang into the air. She
grabbed a rope hanging from a
pulley, then dropped to the deck.
Fez joined her, and they both
pulled on the rope.

They hauled Mr Pickles out of the water. The young monkey wore a diving suit and held what he thought was an old pitchfork. Shells and seaweed covered the long tool.

When Mr Pickles was safely on deck, he pulled off his helmet. The other monkeys marched up to him.

"Did you find any treasure?" asked the captain.

"No, sir." Mr Pickles shook his head. "But I did find this old pitchfork. I used it to look under rocks."

Banana Beard shook his head. "This won't do. This won't do."

He turned to Fez. "I need a volunteer from the crew to search some more," the captain said.

"Aye, Captain," Fez replied. He turned to Fossey. "We need a volunteer from the crew."

Fossey turned to Mr Pickles. "Any volunteers?" she asked.

Mr Pickles looked around. There was no one left to ask.

"I . . . volunteer?" he said.

"There's a good lad," said the captain.

"Aye-aye, Captain," Mr Pickles said. He stood at attention and tapped the pitchfork on the deck.

Just then, the shells and seaweed fell away from the pitchfork. It gleamed in the bright sunlight.

Mr Pickles' eyes widened. He cried, "I've found some treasure, Captain!"

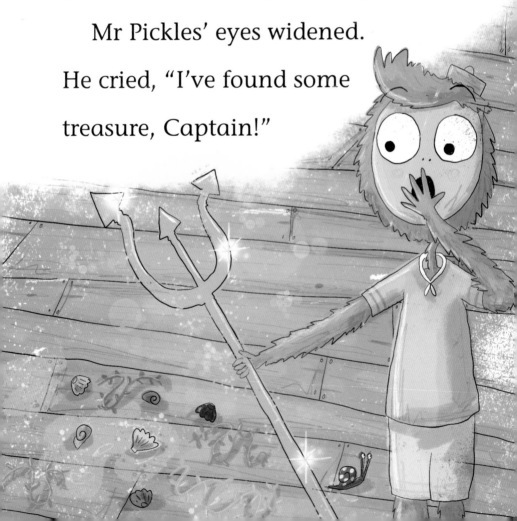

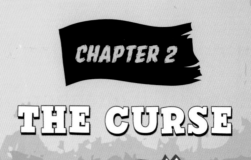

CHAPTER 2

THE CURSE

"Think of all the bananas I can buy with this!" said Captain Banana Beard. He held the pitchfork in one hand and the ship's wheel with the other.

Fez ran up with a dusty old book. "According to *The Pirate Treasure Guide,* that's not a pitchfork – it's Neptune's trident," Fez said. "It's made of solid gold."

"Wonderful!" said the captain.

"And it's cursed," Fez added.

Suddenly a mighty storm formed over the pirate ship. The sky grew dark. Rain poured onto the decks. Wind whipped the sails. Huge waves tossed the ship about.

"Yep, cursed," Fez repeated.

"Cursed, you say?" asked the captain. He gripped the trident and looked up at the clouds. "I've been in worse storms, mateys," he shouted. "This be nothing but drizzle."

"Are you sure this isn't the curse, Captain?" asked Fossey.

KRAK-BOOM!

Lightning struck the water right next to the ship.

"A bunch of yo-ho-hocus-pocus, if you ask me," Banana Beard replied.

Suddenly strange creatures climbed aboard the ship. They had the heads and arms of monkeys but the tails of fish.

"Mermaids," said Fossey.

"Monkey mermaids!" Fez added.

"Mermaids?" Captain Banana Beard asked. He marched down to the main deck. "I get along quite well with mermaids."

KRAK-BOOM!

The next flash of lightning showed more of the mermaids. They had pale skin with glowing red eyes. Jagged teeth filled their mouths. Each fingertip ended with a sharp claw.

"Captain Banana Beard, those aren't normal mermaids," said Fossey. "Those are zombie mermaids!"

The zombie mermaids hissed as more climbed over the side. As they crawled closer, their mouths snapped open and shut.

"They look hungry," said Mr Pickles.

"Give them some bananas," said the captain. "We'll get plenty more when I sell the trident."

"Zombie mermaids don't eat bananas," Fossey explained. "They eat monkey brains."

Mr Pickles rubbed his head. "I don't want them to eat my brain," he said. "I'm still using it."

Captain Banana Beard gulped. "It's all right, mateys," he said. "I have a plan."

"Yes, Captain?" asked Fossey.

". . . **RUN!**"

CHAPTER 3
PLAN B

The monkey pirates scattered, but there was nowhere to hide. Several more zombie mermaids slowly climbed onto the ship. The creatures flopped, slithered and crawled towards the pirates.

"Whoa!" Fez shouted. He dodged a mermaid's sharp claws.

"Aargh!" shouted Fossey. She bounded over two hissing mermaids.

"My brain!" shouted Mr Pickles. He covered his head and ducked as a mermaid flew over him.

Soon the pirates crowded together at the centre of the ship. The zombie mermaids closed in.

"Argh," growled the captain. "I've had second thoughts on me plan." He turned to Fez. "Now, where be those black bananas?"

Fez tapped a nearby barrel. "Right here, Captain."

"Right. Time for plan B," said the captain. "I'm sure these rotten beasties will eat some rotten fruit."

Fez sighed. "Aye-aye, Captain,"
he said, pulling off the barrel lid.
A swarm of fruit flies flew out.
The insects buzzed over the stinky
barrel.

"All right, mateys." The captain
nodded. "Off you go."

Fez, Fossey and Mr Pickles each held their breath. They reached into the barrel. They grabbed fistfuls of stinky, squishy black bananas.

The three monkeys flung them at the zombie mermaids.

SPLAT!

FWOP!

FWAP!

The rotten fruit smacked against the mermaids. The creatures didn't seem to care. They crawled closer.

"Begging the captain's pardon," said Mr Pickles, "but would you happen to have a plan C?"

CHAPTER 4

PLAN C?

"Aye! I do have a plan C," Captain Banana Beard said. "As in, see who can get to the top of the ship first!"

The captain scrambled up the ropes of the main mast. The other monkeys followed him up the tall pole at the centre of the ship.

The monkeys made it all the way to the crow's nest on top of the mast.

They crowded inside the small basket and looked down.

All the zombie mermaids climbed up after them. The creatures hissed as they closed in.

"What now, Captain?" asked Fossey.

"Fear not," Banana Beard said. "I have a plan . . . where was I?"

"Plan D, sir?" Fez asked.

"Quite right," said the captain. He handed the trident to Fez. "Hold this."

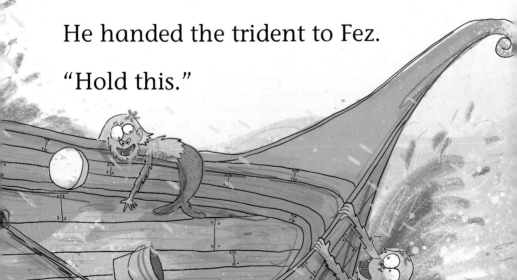

The captain reached up and grabbed a rope leading to the back of the ship. He swung out of the crow's nest and slid down the rope.

"OK," said Fez. He turned to Fossey. "Hold this."

Fez gave Fossey the trident and then slid down the rope after the captain.

"Here," said Fossey. She handed the trident to Mr Pickles. Then she followed Fez down the rope.

Mr Pickles was all alone.

"Just slide on down, lad!"
shouted the captain. "And don't
forget me trident."

Mr Pickles shivered as he
gripped the trident. The zombie
mermaids were almost on top
of him!

Mr Pickles gulped. "Oh, dear."

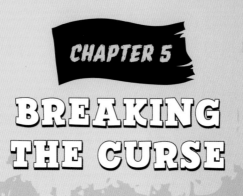

CHAPTER 5

BREAKING THE CURSE

Mr Pickles couldn't decide how to grab the rope *and* hold onto the trident.

Finally, he swung the trident over the rope. He grabbed the handle from each side. Then he used the trident to slide down.

"Now why didn't I think of that?" asked Captain Banana Beard.

One of the mermaids flew out from the pack. She grabbed the rope below Mr Pickles. He was sliding right towards her biting teeth!

SNAP! Just then, the rope snapped beneath them.

Mr Pickles let go of the trident and grabbed for the rope. He latched on and held tight.

Unfortunately, he swung back towards the rest of the zombie mermaids. Mr Pickles shut his eyes tight. He landed on the mast – right in the middle of the hungry creatures.

"Mr Pickles!" shouted Fossey.

"Mr Pickles!" shouted Fez.

"Me trident!" shouted Captain
Banana Beard.

The captain watched the golden trident tumble through the air.

Flying over the side of the boat, it splashed into the sea.

PLUNK!

Suddenly the rain stopped. The dark clouds disappeared. And the mermaids fell away from the mast.

Some jumped into the water. Some landed on the deck. Most importantly, they were no longer zombies.

Mr Pickles hung upside down on the mast. His eyes were still shut tight. He covered his head with both hands.

He opened one eye and felt his head. "Oh, good." He sighed with relief. "My brain is still there."

The last of the mermaids paused before she climbed over the side. "Thank you, Captain," she said. "You saved my sisters and me from the terrible curse."

"Uh . . . yes . . . ," the captain said nervously. Then he bowed deeply. "All part of me plan, dear lady. All part of me plan."

"I wonder which plan that was?" Fez asked Fossey.

After the last mermaid had gone, the captain pulled a banana from his beard. He took a bite and looked around.

"Well then," he said. "We seem to be fresh out of treasure." He turned to the others. "First Mate Fez, I need a volunteer from the crew to search for more."

Fez turned to Fossey. "We need a volunteer."

Fossey turned to Mr Pickles. He was already climbing into the diving suit.

Mr Pickles sighed. "I . . . I volunteer."

Captain Banana Beard raised a finger. "You know . . . I've just realized something."

Mr Pickles smiled. "You've realized that seeking treasure isn't worth the risk?" he asked. "And the true treasure is right here on this ship? The true treasure is our friendships?"

Banana Beard smiled and patted
Mr Pickles on the shoulder.

Then he burst into laughter.
"Good one, lad!" he cried.

The captain finally finished
laughing. "No, you forgot this,"
he said.

Captain Banana Beard handed Mr Pickles *The Pirate Treasure Guide* book. "No more cursed treasure," he said. "Captain's orders."

Mr Pickles sighed. "Aye-aye, Captain." He took the book and put on his diving helmet.

Rummmble...

Thunder rumbled in the distance.

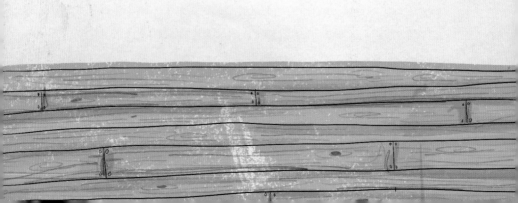

ABOUT THE AUTHOR

Michael Anthony Steele has been in the entertainment industry for more than twenty years. He has worked in several capacities of film and television production from props and special effects all the way up to writing and directing. For many years, Michael has written exclusively for family entertainment, including several children's television series. He has written more than one hundred books for various characters and brands, including *Batman*, *Green Lantern*, *LEGO City*, *Spider-Man*, *The Hardy Boys*, *Garfield* and *Night at the Museum*.

ABOUT THE ILLUSTRATOR

Pauline Reeves lives by the sea in south-west England, with her husband, two children and her dog, Jenson. She has loved drawing and creating since she was a child. Following her passion, Pauline graduated from Plymouth College of Art with a degree in illustration, and she specializes in children's literature. She takes inspiration from the funny and endearing things animals and people do every day. Pauline works both digitally and with traditional materials to create quirky illustrations full of humour and charm.

GLOSSARY

curse spell intended to harm someone by calling on evil spirits or powers

jagged with sharp, uneven points sticking out

mast tall pole at the centre of a boat or ship that holds up one or more sails

pitchfork large fork with a long handle, used for lifting and moving hay on farms

risk possibility of loss or harm; danger

scallywag someone who is naughty or full of mischief

scramble crawl or climb in a hurried way, using hands and feet

trident spear that has three points and that looks like a large fork

volunteer someone who offers to do a job

1. Have you ever volunteered to do something? How did it feel? Do you think Mr Pickles likes to volunteer for jobs on the ship?

2. In your opinion, is Captain Banana Beard a good captain? Why or why not?

3. Captain Banana Beard is searching for treasure. What is one of your most treasured possessions? How did you get it?

FOR YOUR PIRATE LOG

1. The Captain has a lot of plans (A, B, C and even D) for how to save the crew from the zombie mermaids, but none of them work. Write what plan E could have been if Mr Pickles hadn't saved the day.

2. Write a list of things you think a zombie mermaid does in a typical day.

3. Mr Pickles saved the crew by throwing the trident overboard. Think of a time you had an idea that helped your friends or family. Write a sentence or two describing how you saved the day.